EAH... UT WE ON'T KNOW HO TOOK IT. PRINCIPAL ARKER FINDS UT...

UT SHE'S OT GOING O FIND UT...

...IS SHE?

YOU TELL ME.

THERE IS A LOGICAL SUSPECT WHO REEKED OF GUILT!

I-DIDN'T-DO-IT-! NOBODY-SAW-ME-! YOU-CAN'T-PROVE-A-THING-!

ATTENDING PRAYER CLUB THAT DAY WAS LIKE WEARING A BIG "GUILTY" SIGN!

YOU'RE BLACKMAILING ME!

BLACK FEMALING YOU, ACTUALLY. BUT YOU GET MY POINT.

BUT...

...START ATTENDING REGULARLY, THEN MAYBE YOU DON'T LOOK QUITE SO GUILTY.

MY FOLKS FINALLY FOUND OUT WHEN I HAD A BAD BIKE ACCIDENT.

THANK GOD THEY SENT ME TO REHAB INSTEAD OF DENYING MY PROBLEM!

I'VE BEEN COMING TO THESE MEETINGS EVER SINCE.

WHAT ABOUT YOUR FRIEND?

HE'S DEAD.

The 12 Steps

Here are the steps we took, which are suggested as a program of recovery:

1. We admitted we were powerless over drugs and alcohol, that our lives had become unmanageable.

2. Came to believe that a Power greater than ourselves could restore us to sanity.

3. Made a decision to turn our will and our lives over to the care of God as we understood Him.

4. Made a searching and fearless moral inventory of ourselves.

5. Admitted to God, to ourselves, and to another human being the exact nature of our wrongs.

6. Were entirely ready to have God remove all these defects of character.

7. Humbly asked Him to remove our shortcomings.

8. Made a list of all persons we had harmed, and became willing to make amends to them all.

9. Made direct amends to such people wherever possible, except when to do so would injure them or others.

10. Continued to take personal inventory and when we were wrong promptly admitted it.

11. Sought through prayer and meditation to improve our conscious contact with God as we understood Him, praying only for knowledge of His will for us and the power to carry that out.

12. Having had a spiritual awakening as the result of these steps, we tried to carry this message to others, and to practice these principles in all our affairs.

-- Based on the AA Big Book

YOU'VE BEEN WARNED BEFORE!

YOU CAN BE **SEVERELY DISCIPLINED** IF YOU PRACTICE RELIGION DURING SCHOOL!

I CAN'T TALK ABOUT RELIGION AT SCHOOL -- SEPARATION OF CHURCH AND STATE.

BUT...

IF WE **BOTH** STEP ON THE SIDEWALK, WE'RE **OFF SCHOOL GROUNDS.**

WHAT'S PRAYING ALL ABOUT? IS THERE SOME SPECIFIC RITUAL?

NOT REALLY.

SO WHAT DO I SAY? WHAT DO I PRAY ABOUT? AND WHERE?

FIND A QUIET PLACE AND SAY WHAT'S ON YOUR HEART.

I THINK THIS IS THE WAY THEY DO IT ON TV.

YOU LEFT YOUR --

?????

WHAT ARE YOU DOING?

-- UH -- NOTHING! JUST LOOKING FOR SOMETHING UNDER MY BED!

NO PRIVACY HERE...BETTER GO OUT...

OKAY, NOBODY'S LOOKING, SO NOBODY'S GONNA LAUGH!

NOW I CAN PRAY!

"OH LORD, HALLOWEDLY WE BESEECH THEE TO BLESSEDLY BESTOWETH --"

YEESH! THAT SOUNDS STUPID!

IF IT WON'T CHEESE YOU, I'M JUST GONNA TALK TO YOU, 'KAY?

NO THUNDERBOLTS. SO FAR, SO GOOD.

meep meep

DAD LET ME BUY A CAR!

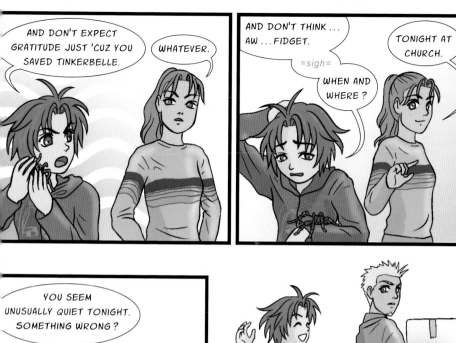

BETTER MAKE SURE SHE DOESN'T TAKE ANY SIDE TRIPS!

YO! SERENITY! WAIT UP!

DAD SAID DON'T LET ANYBODY ELSE DRIVE.

STILL, WHAT COULD GO WRONG?

ska-

REEEECH!

UH-OH!
YOU JUST HIT
OFFICER
CHERRYTOP!

*not to be confused with Narconon

Chapter

THERE'S A REASON AND A PURPOSE BEHIND EVERYTHING THE PRAYER CLUB DOE... HERE'S WHERE THEY FIND GUIDANCE AND MEANING FOR THEIR LIVES:

"DO NOT BE DECEIVED: GOD CANNOT BE MOCKED. A MAN REAPS WHAT HE SOWS."

Galatians 6:7 (New International Version)

"THEREFORE CONFESS YOUR SINS TO EACH OTHER AND PRAY FOR EACH OTHER SO THAT YOU MAY BE HEALED. THE PRAYER OF A RIGHTEOUS MAN IS POWERFUL AND EFFECTIVE."

James 5:16 (NIV)

"THIS IS THE CONFIDENCE WE HAVE IN APPROACHING GOD: THAT IF WE ASK ANYTHING ACCORDING TO HIS WILL, HE HEARS US."

1 John 5:14 (NIV)

and Verse

"CARRY EACH OTHER'S
BURDENS, AND IN THIS WAY
YOU WILL FULFILL THE LAW
OF CHRIST."

Galatians 6:2 (NIV)

"LOVE YOUR ENEMIES AND
PRAY FOR THOSE WHO
PERSECUTE YOU."

Matthew 5:44 (NIV)

"DO TO OTHERS AS YOU WOULD
HAVE THEM DO TO YOU."

Luke 6:31 (NIV)

BOTTOM LINE:
"O YOU WHO HEAR PRAYER, TO YOU ALL MEN WILL COME.
WHEN WE WERE OVERWHELMED BY SINS, YOU FORGAVE OUR TRANSGRESSIONS."

Psalm 65:2-3 (NIV)

Sign up for e-mail news at

www.serenitybuzz.com

- ◎ **Get downloads**
- ◎ **Chat with the author**
- ◎ **Preview upcoming books**
- ◎ **Meet the characters**

THE PEOPLE BEHIND THE SCENES. . .

BUZZ DIXON is the founder of Realbuzz Studios. A veteran of the comic and cartoon industry, Buzz has worked with Stan Lee of Marvel Comics, and on numerous projects ranging from Precious Moments to Tiny Toons to G. I. Joe. Buzz and his family live in southern California.

MIN "KEIIII" KWON is responsible for penciling and inking Serenity. Although primarily a manga illustrator, the recent Rutgers graduate works in many different forms of visual art.

Serenity's Story CONTINUES!

olume 3,
asket Case

Available
arch 2006

Serenity laughs at responsibility.

But there's nothing funny about this job. . . .

The prayer club's pet project is at her irresponsible best, belittling a health class assignment that makes teens care for chicken eggs 24/7 to simulate the work a baby requires. But when an overwhelming responsibility falls upon Serenity, where can she get help—from the friends she's made fun of, or the God she doesn't quite believe exists?

Future titles:

Rave and Rant—Available May 2006
Snow Biz—Available July 2006
You Shall Love—Available September 2006

SERENITY

ART BY MIN KWON
CREATED BY BUZZ DIXON
ORIGINAL CHARACTER DESIGNS
BY DRIGZ ABROT

SERENITY THROWS A BIG WET SLOPPY ONE OUT TO:
STEF D. AND ALL OF BILL W.'S FRIENDS.

LUV U GUYZ !!!

©&TM 2005 by Realbuzz Studios   ISBN 1-59310-942-3

Published by Barbour Publishing, Inc., P.O. Box 719, Uhrichsville, Ohio 44683
www.barbourbooks.com

"OUR MISSION IS TO PUBLISH AND DISTRIBUTE
INSPIRATIONAL PRODUCTS OFFERING EXCEPTIONAL VALUE
AND BIBLICAL ENCOURAGEMENT TO THE MASSES."

 Member of the
Evangelical Christian
Publishers Association

Scripture quotations marked NIV are taken from
The Holy Bible, New International Version®. NIV®.
Copyright © 1973, 1978, 1984 by International Bible Society.
Used by permission of Zondervan. All rights reserved.

Printed in China.
5 4 3 2 1

VISIT SERENITY AT:
www.Serenitybuzz.com
www.RealbuzzStudios.com